KU-254-645

HM

3 1 MAY 2024

WITHDRAWN

R hts

Get **more** out of libraries

Please return or renew this item by the last date shown.
You can renew online at www.hants.gov.uk/library
r by phoning   0300 555 1387

Hampshire
County Council

C016112756

This Faber book belongs to

....

*For my brother, with love and thanks for
making my childhood unforgettable*
C.R.

First published in the UK in 2015
by Faber and Faber Ltd,
Bloomsbury House,
74–77 Great Russell Street, London WC1B 3DA

The text was first published as the poem
'The Ride-by-Nights' in Walter de la Mare's
Peacock Pie poetry collection in 1913.

Printed in China

Text © The Literary Trustees of Walter de la Mare, 1969
Illustrations © Carolina Rabei, 2015

A CIP record for this book is available
from the British Library

HB ISBN 978–0–571–32422–4
PB ISBN 978–0–571–30719–7

10 9 8 7 6 5 4 3 2 1

All rights reserved

FSC
www.fsc.org

MIX
Paper from
responsible sources
FSC® C020056

The Ride-by-Nights

Walter de la Mare

Illustrated by Carolina Rabei

ff

FABER & FABER

Up on their brooms the Witches stream,

Crooked and black in the crescent's gleam;

One foot high,

and one foot low,

Bearded, cloaked, and cowled, they go.

'Neath Charlie's Wain they twitter and tweet,

And away they swarm 'neath the Dragon's feet,

With a whoop and a flutter
they swing and sway,

And surge pell-mell
down the Milky Way.

Between the legs of the glittering Chair
They hover and squeak in the empty air.

Then round they swoop past the glimmering Lion

To where Sirius barks behind huge Orion;

Up, then, and over to wheel amain,

Under the silver,

and home again.